FAVOURITE CLASSICS
OLIVER TWIST

Retold by Sasha Morton

Illustrated by Jon Mitchell

Ticktock

An Hachette UK Company
www.hachette.co.uk

First published in Great Britain in 2014 by Ticktock,
an imprint of Octopus Publishing Group Ltd
Endeavour House
189 Shaftesbury Avenue
London
WC2H 8JY
www.octopusbooks.co.uk
www.ticktockbooks.co.uk

ISBN 978 1 84898 930 6

A CIP record for this book is available from the British Library.

Printed and bound in China

10 9 8 7 6 5 4 3 2 1

Series Editor: Lucy Cuthew Design: Advocate Art
Publisher: Tim Cook Managing Editor: Karen Rigden
Production Controller: Sarah Connelly

Contents

The Characters

Oliver

Nancy

Fagin

Oliver's Mother's Locket

The Artful Dodger

Mr Bumble

Bill Sikes

Mr Brownlow

Chapter 1
Oliver Twist is Born

On a dark night, in a workhouse for homeless women, a baby boy was born. As the child was wrapped in a grubby blanket, his mother let out her last breath.

And in that very moment, a servant noticed the dead woman's valuable locket, and stole it.

Any chance of finding the newborn boy's family seemed lost forever.

So the child was sent to an orphanage, where he was named Oliver Twist by Mr Bumble, the man who was in charge of looking after the poor and homeless people in the town.

Oliver lived in the orphanage until he was three years old, but soon he was moved to a place known as The Farm. There Oliver wore dirty, torn clothes and had to survive on the smallest meals you could imagine.

Yet as bad as it was there, the weeks turned into years and Oliver settled into his new life and even had a few friends.

But on Oliver's ninth birthday, Mr Bumble appeared again.
This time he was taking Oliver somewhere
to be dreaded and feared...

the workhouse.

Oliver Twist had never known such hunger. He ate just one ladle of gruel each day. His face was pale and his clothes had become even looser on his thin body.

At supper one evening, the other starving boys persuaded Oliver to ask for an extra ration of gruel, **even though they knew it was forbidden.**

Slowly, Oliver walked to where the master stood.

Taking a deep breath,
Oliver held up his empty bowl
and said in a brave voice,

"Please, Sir, I want some more."

The room fell silent. The boys held their breath.
"What?" whispered the master in disbelief.
"Please, sir," repeated Oliver nervously. "I want some more."

With that, the master hit Oliver with his ladle and shouted for Mr Bumble to take him away.

Poor Oliver! Within moments, Mr Bumble had locked him in a dark, stone cell and posted a notice on the door of the workhouse.

NOTICE

The parish offers a reward to any person who needs an apprentice.

Please ask inside about Oliver Twist.

After a miserable week alone in his cell, Oliver was marched into town to meet his new master.

"This is your home now, Oliver," announced Mr Bumble cheerfully.

"The parish has paid three pounds to be rid of a naughty orphan no one can love. Goodbye."

"I will be good, sir," called Oliver to the departing Mr Bumble.

His hopeful words went unheard.

SOWERBERRY UNDERTAKERS

That morning, little Oliver Twist began his working life.
By day, he helped carry out funerals.

By night, he slept in one of the coffins his master had built.

But an older servant boy kept bullying Oliver,
so one foggy night Oliver made a big decision
that would change his life for ever. **He ran away.**

Chapter 2
Fagin's Den

Oliver walked for miles. It took several days before he finally staggered into London, exhausted. Grateful to have reached the city at last, he sat down to rest his tired feet.

Soon, a young lad who had been watching Oliver approached him. "What's your name then?" he enquired cheerfully. "I'm Jack Dawkins, but everyone calls me the Artful Dodger."

"I'm Oliver Twist," said Oliver. "Are there any cheap lodgings near here? Not that I have any money to pay for them just yet."

A grin spread slowly across the Artful Dodger's face as he replied, "There most certainly are. Follow me!"

"Fagin!" bellowed Dodger as he shoved
Oliver up a flight of dark stairs.
"Meet our new friend!"

A shabby old man peered at Oliver and cackled,
"Welcome, young man.
We are happy to share what
little we have with you."

Fagin's home was black with dirt and filled to the brim with noisy lads. As a space was cleared for Oliver to sleep in, there was a loud knock at the door and Oliver saw Fagin quickly hide a large box in one of the rafters.

"Bill! Nancy!" cried Fagin. "Come and meet Oliver Twist."

Oliver didn't like the way Bill stared at him but Nancy gave him a warm hug.

What a strange new world I have entered, thought Oliver.

As the days passed, Oliver learned more about his new friends. Fagin had taught all of his boys to steal wallets and handkerchiefs for him to sell. Now he taught these tricks to Oliver, who thought it all just a jolly game.

When his new master patted him on the head and called him a **"clever boy"** for being such a quick learner, Oliver glowed with pride.

Before long, Oliver was desperate to spend some time outside Fagin's grubby den. After much pleading, the old man agreed to let Oliver go to work with the Artful Dodger the next day.

Oliver watched as Dodger reached into an elderly man's pocket. Dodger had no sooner ducked out of sight than the man noticed his handkerchief was gone. His eyes landed on young Oliver, who suddenly realised his new friend was a thief.

In a panic, Oliver fled.

"Stop thief!"
shouted the old man.

Oliver ran as fast as his innocent legs could carry him. On and on he raced through the crowded streets, then…

THUD!

…he was caught.

Chapter 3
Mr Brownlow

Oliver's legs shook as he stood nervously in the dock at the local courthouse.

"Oliver Twist,
I find you guilty of theft,"
boomed the judge.

Oliver gasped.
He was going to prison!

Just then, the courtroom door flew open and
the bookstall owner rushed up to the dock.

"I saw the boy who stole from
Mr Brownlow, your Honour.
It's not this lad here."

With that, Oliver began to wobble...
the room began to spin...
and everything
went black.

When Oliver awoke, he found himself in a clean, warm bed.

"Where am I?" he whispered.

An elderly woman wiped his head with a cloth and replied, "Hush, my dear. You have been very ill, you must rest."

Over the following days, Oliver learned that Mr Brownlow had been so worried about what would become of him after he fainted that he'd brought him to his own home to recover.

Mrs Bedwin, his housekeeper, had nursed him back to health.

But outside, two shadowy figures watched the house and waited…

As the weeks went by, Oliver grew well and strong in his new home. Mr Brownlow even began to teach him to read and write.

Life had never been so good.

One day, as the housekeeper brought Oliver his afternoon tea, Mr Brownlow let out a gasp.

"Mrs Bedwin, look at that!" he cried, pointing to the painting behind Oliver's head. "They could be the same person!"

Mrs Bedwin and Oliver looked up at the painting. Mr Brownlow's niece had run away over eight years ago, yet her eyes, nose, lips… were identical to Oliver's.

The next morning, Oliver noticed the painting was gone.

One afternoon, Mr Brownlow asked Oliver to run an errand for him. "Oliver, please take these books back to the market for me and return with some new ones. Come back with ten shillings change," instructed Mr Brownlow.

"Yes, sir!" called Oliver cheerfully.

A visiting friend of Mr Brownlow's looked at Oliver suspiciously as he left. "I'll bet that's the last you'll see of the boy and your money," he laughed.

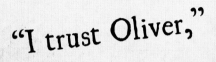

"I trust Oliver," stated Mr Brownlow firmly, "and I intend to find his real family. He'll be back soon, you wait and see."

But Oliver did not return.

Chapter 4
The Robbery

"Get off me! Leave me alone!" cried Oliver. He tried to run but Bill's dirty hand gripped him tightly.

"No chance," Bill growled. "You could lead the police straight to Fagin and his stash of stolen gold. Besides, you're just the right size to help me with a robbery I'm planning."

Bill dragged Oliver all the way back to Fagin's den and locked him in the attic.

Until one night he came for him...

33

Bill took Oliver to a grand country house.

"You're small enough to get through there," Bill said, pointing to an unlocked window at the back of the house. "Once you're in, unlock the front door so I can get in and grab their silver. If you do what I say, I might let you live."

Fearfully, Oliver did as Bill demanded. The floorboards creaked as he crept across the room. It seemed everyone was asleep until…

CRACK!

…a gun was fired.

Hearing the gunshot, Bill sprinted away without a backward glance. Oliver must be dead, and dead boys couldn't tell the police where thieves live, could they?

For many days and nights after he was shot, Oliver suffered from a fever. Hour by hour, the women of the house prayed for the boy to live…

In the care of Mrs Maylie, and her daughter Rose, Oliver began to recover. As spring turned to summer, they pieced together everything that had happened in Oliver's short life.

"As soon as you are well enough we will take you to Mr Brownlow, Oliver," said Rose. "The police can deal with Fagin and Bill Sikes."

But Fagin himself had been spying on the house and was shocked to discover that Oliver was still alive.

It was time for Bill Sikes to deal with Oliver Twist once and for all...

Meanwhile, Mr Brownlow was determined to solve the mystery of both the missing boy and his lost niece. He had written to the workhouse where Oliver had been born and Mr Bumble had agreed to visit him.

"This Mr Brownlow seems a wealthy man," said Mr Bumble greedily. "He might pay us for any information we can provide about that dirty little orphan."

"Or for this," cackled Mrs Bumble, holding up the stolen locket that had belonged to Oliver's mother. "I was lucky to find it when that thieving old servant died."

Feeling very important, the Bumbles watched
Mr Brownlow examine the locket.

"You say the woman who stole this
from my runaway niece died years
ago?" asked Mr Brownlow slowly.

"Yes indeed, sir!"
answered Mr Bumble
brightly. But he quickly
realised his mistake…

"So you kept the one thing that could have returned Oliver to his real family?" shouted Mr Brownlow.

"Get out of my house and don't come back!"

As the door slammed loudly behind the fleeing Bumbles, Mr Brownlow stared out of the window and wondered where in the world his great-nephew could be.

Chapter 5
To London Bridge

As dusk fell in London, Oliver and Rose Maylie's carriage drew up outside Mr Brownlow's house. Nancy watched Rose knock on the door and saw Oliver's face fall when there was no reply.

"We'll return tomorrow, Oliver," said Rose kindly. "One more night won't make any difference."

Yes it will, thought Nancy. She knew that Bill intended to snatch Oliver back as soon as he could. This time, he wouldn't let the boy live to tell the police about Bill's crimes. Nancy knew it was up to her to stop his terrible plan.

Quickly, she pushed a note through Mr Brownlow's letterbox.

Oliver is back. He is in danger.

Meet me at London Bridge at midnight. We must save the boy from Bill Sikes.

A friend

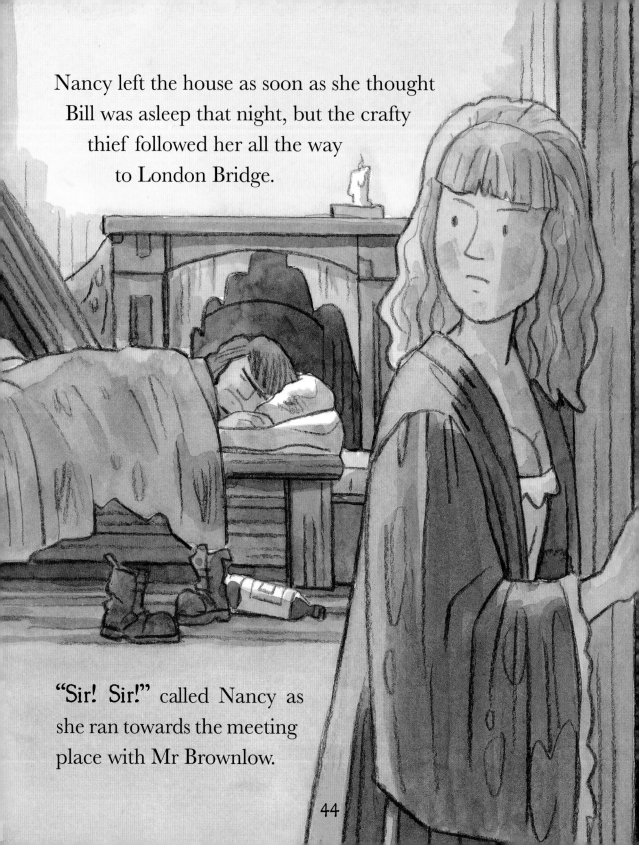

Nancy left the house as soon as she thought Bill was asleep that night, but the crafty thief followed her all the way to London Bridge.

"Sir! Sir!" called Nancy as she ran towards the meeting place with Mr Brownlow.

44

He heard Nancy's shout and ran down the steps to the riverbank, only to find her lying dead on the ground. Bill's murderous footsteps echoed loudly as he fled into a dark alleyway.

"After him!" shouted Mr Brownlow to a nearby policeman. Within minutes, a sea of people surged behind Bill as he ran for his life.

Panting, Bill locked himself in Fagin's old den.

"We've got you trapped," yelled the waiting police.

Determined to escape, Bill climbed out onto the slippery roof. A crowd had gathered and they watched as he lost his footing once… twice… then toppled backwards onto the stone cobbles far below. **It was all over.**

What became of Fagin, you may ask. Unfortunately for him, the police had become extremely good at catching pickpockets.

Before long, both Fagin and the Artful Dodger began new lives behind bars.

They often wondered whatever became of the little orphan boy called Oliver Twist…

When Rose, Mrs Maylie and Oliver arrived at Mr Brownlow's house the next day, Oliver received the warmest homecoming an orphan could ever dream of.

"Welcome back, Oliver," said Mr Brownlow happily. "Our family is complete."

Oliver realised all of the danger and loneliness of his childhood was finally over.

He was home!